THE SLEEPERS

and

A MIDSUMMER DAY'S DREAM

MARSHALL JAMES KAVANAUGH

spread it

A FREEDOM BOOK

A FREEDOM BOOKS PRODUCTION
Published by Willow Zef
Willow Zef — zefm@comcast.net

Copyright © Marshall James Kavanaugh, 2012
The Sleepers was previously published in *subtext Magazine* © Pharaoh Quintessential, 2012
A Midsummer Day's Dream is previously unpublished but is part of a broader
collection.

LIBRARY OF CONGRESS CATALOGUING IN PUBLICATION DATA
Kavanaugh, Marshall James, 1987-
The Sleepers and A Midsummer Day's Dream / Marshall James Kavanaugh
p. cm.
ISBN 978 0 615 926 24 7
1.   Kavanaugh, Marshall James, 1987- -Biography.   2. Authors, American—
21st century—biography
1.   Title

Printed in the United States of America

marshall.kavanaugh@gmail.com
http://www.marshalljameskavanaugh.com

Contents

Acknowledgements   vii

Introduction   ix

Author's Note   xiii

The Sleepers   1
A Midsummer Day's Dream   27

Acknowledgements

I would like to thank my publisher Willow Zef for encouraging me to put out my first book as well as giving me a vehicle to carry it to new readers and new dreamers on A Freedom Books,

My colleague A Augustus Depenbrock for warming my spirits with fresh whimsical collaboration and the sharp words of an editor's tongue,

And Sophie C. White for having the beauty and influence of a muse in and out of my waking life.

I would like to co-dedicate this book to my parents for their ongoing support of my eccentricities and to Mike Hall whose short life still has a strong effect on me to this day, with his humble nature and "Hey, brother" always in my waking thoughts.

Introduction

Two trapeze artists swing from one end of the tent to the other spinning through the air tumbling and twirling as if they were swimming in an ocean so graceful. The audience looks on in pure childlike amusement mouths open wide in awe and near disbelief. What capabilities have they! to be moving through the air like acrobatic fish.

Welcome To The Mind Of Marshall James Kavanaugh says a sign at the tent entrance. A man standing yelling through a megaphone booms, "Welcome! one and all!"

There are many acts to follow:
the lion tamers who boldly place their
bodies within the jowls of those ter-
rible African beasts, the contortionists who fold their bodies into unrec-
ognizable positions, and for those with
courage in their hearts, there are the
grotesque spectacles of the freak show
and the bearded lady, the man with two
heads and the little wolf-boy.

But of course! his mind is not
limited to the fantasies within the
tent, oh no, the genius of James Kavanaugh spills out to the travelling
hands washing the elephants and the
caravan full of gypsies predicting the
future with crystal ball prophecies and
tarot card visions.

And even beyond the lay of the *carnival de fantastique*, the nearby city and village are astir with excitement and frenzy, the conversations in the cafes are spurred on by the pure absurdity of one man coming to town and popping a circus from his crown chakra. How can this be? they ask. Is it true? Have you seen?

After prolonged hours and weeks of whimsies and delights, James Kavanaugh packs up his theatrics and the people awaken as if from a slumber unsure the source of their experience. Waking life? Sleeping dreams?

He smiles and laughs and motions with his arms, this dreamer of dream laborers, writing his stories without a pen painting pictures with a sensuous language rolling off of the tongue, he creates beauty of madness and madness and love, the truest of dream poets, I am honored to open these pages for what is to come: brilliance, magic, and what is better than that? Simply said, and in all earnest, ready yourself for a truly authentic mind.

Willow Zef
Philadelphia
October 2012

Author's Note

The stories contained in this collection are not based on any dream I have ever dreamt and yet they feel fresh and new and real to me as if I had just lived in them the night before last. They are dreams that I dream of having if only my doors of perception were opened a little wider and the weirdness within was brought into full focus. There is no moral of the story or lesson to be learned there is only the glow of a heightened experience and the joy that frolics out from within. There are characters and experiences to be had in a setting that is free from the restraints of a real world.

The reader should be warned though the warning is not of imminent danger. Reading these tales will lead to dreams of wonderful and extravagant nature. A world where contortionists twist themselves into letters and write green poetry for young soft maidens while tall strapping trumpet players stand and play the horn they were born with coming in fine musical notes in perfect harmony with one another. There is much lust and love in this world that the reader will find themselves in and it is there that they will learn that they are one with their human nature. With their eyes closed they will see all that is beautiful and all that can be in a world based on their dreams.

Many writers have attempted the work of dream laboring before to name a few contemporaries Henry Miller Jack Kerouac William S Burroughs and even William Blake so these stories are only as unique as the pen that first wrote them but they do come from the heart and a certain manifestation that I have not yet quite figured out but often think of as some type of possession or the channeling of a long dead voice who wants to live and fuck again like old times. This is where the magic from these stories comes in and the sometimes distant frame of reference as if the narrator was an omnipotent third eye.

These stories work in the same universe as a yet to be published novel titled *Pharaoh Quintessential's Grand Salon*. I have never written anything like this before and though I have always been interested in dreams and their content my attempts at a dream sequence before these works has always been a bit forced. I attribute my travels to Spain as having a significant impact on both my style and playfulness in language as it is right after I returned to Philadelphia that I first experienced the creep over my shoulders of someone or something else controlling my hands and writing out the stories with me just as a body to maneuver through each word. This combined with the sublime surreal

madness I have gained by living in Philadelphia for the last few years of my
twenty something life has lead to this
new definition I have for what it means
to write.

You can look into my life and you
can look for them but none of these
characters exist in our plane of life
nor have I met them in any way shape or
form and yet they are as real as you
or I playing singing fucking enjoying
dancing sleeping and dreaming and living like the noble souls that they have
manifested themselves as constantly
creating and working through their day
to day lives. We can peer in but only
for brief moments and it is with this
we recollect and feel brief breaths of

the genius centered in our own lively minds.

And so it is with that I leave you to enjoy and dream and breath and find yourself in the world of these majestic mirages on the dark cave's old rocky walls.

The Sleepers

Ernesto Alvarez held his left hand to his hip close to where his pistol was fastened in its holster. It stayed there at the ready with only the slightest movement of a finger along the leather grip. With his other hand he held a toothpick to his mouth, which he twirled with his tongue. Ernesto wore dark sunglasses but his presence was loud with his black blazer opened exposing a tie-dyed un-

dershirt. At his left side stood Jane
Claulfield. Her brown hair was held in a
ponytail. She wore a second-hand cock-
tail dress that was a dazzling red of
the old fashion. Her arm was purposely
intertwined with Ernesto's. Groucho Rex
remained behind them two steps to their
right. He was the brawn of the group,
but unlike the rest he had the capabil-
ity to blend in. His gray suit played
well with the cement walls surrounding
them and with his cap lowered to just
above the eyes he felt sure he could not
be seen.

Within the entry hall of the reno-
vated loft space, all attention was directed towards Jasper Jones and Amelia
Alda. Standing at the top of the flight

of stairs each holding a glass of champagne they presented a toast to their guests and patrons.

Ernesto meanwhile turned and nodded towards Groucho for him to take a walk and scope out the rest of the estate. Groucho lit a cigarette and wandered off. Ernesto had Jane by the hand now and squeezed the way he would a child's, removing the toothpick and whispering,

"Come here."

She moved closer to him so that their faces almost met at the nose.

"Do you believe in love at first sight?"

She responded with hesitance so he went on, "I bet you do. You must. I'm sure of it almost. Those pretty eyes have seen love before me."

He tossed the toothpick aside and led her by the hand following the party through the marble doorways into the ballroom. He continued,

"But, have you ever confessed your love to another man?"

Jane let go of his hand and stepped off a little, as if in fright.

"What business do you have asking me a thing like that?"

"There are plenty of pretty girls here tonight, but I only want to be in the company of a woman," he replied.

"Ernesto, you're too serious. You should loosen your belt. Then you would begin to be more than a boy."

He put his arms around her and kissed her. For a moment she let him but then with both hands against his chest she pushed him away from her. As he walked away following the rest of the guests into the ballroom, she put a finger to her lips touching again the sensuous exchange and her eyes gave the hint of a girlish smile.

Music had begun to play in the vein of the eighties no-wave and the majority of guests began to dance with each other. Ernesto stood on the outer edges examining the crowd again with a toothpick in his mouth and a tense hand at his side. A gentleman with a thick mustache dressed in a military uniform approached him and introduced himself.

"Have it here, friend." With a big hand the military gentleman grabbed hold of Ernesto and shook his hand. "The name is Frederick. Sergeant Frederick Clearwater. What's your name, kid?"

"Ernesto Alvarez, but you're no friend of mine that I know."

"Well, Ernesto, I saw in your eyes you had some wit. Have it here, friend. Have this whiskey sour. I would like to tell you about a dream I had two nights prior. Is it alright if I tell you now?"

Ernesto nodded his head saying, "Would you be so kind?"

With that the sergeant launched into a dream sequence describing how he had dreamed himself as a young boy about sixteen years of age standing along the sidewalk of a town he had long forgotten. It was before wartime and his mother was with him, but her attention was directed towards the glass windows of the storefronts and before too long she had entered into one without him. As he stood there waiting for his mother to return, a wonderfully beautiful woman approached him from afar. He watched as she curtsied in his direction and when she was finally next to him she asked if he remembered her. He did but she was not a girl that he would have known at the age of sixteen. No, it was a woman from much later in his life. Maybe twenty years later. He told her he remembered her so as not to keep her waiting, but he asked her what she was doing here now. He was only a boy, couldn't she see that? She said that she could not have waited any longer in the shadows for him. She had decided she must see him now before it would be too late and their chances of being together would have foreclosed. The sky seemed to echo her response as what was a sunny day suddenly turned dismal and gray.

He took the woman's hand and nuzzled it with his chin before kissing each knuckle with eccentric delight. Then he pulled her towards him and wrapped his arms around her bringing her close enough so that he could smell the sweetness of her hair with his head placed upon her shoulder. There they stood for sometime and though it was gray all around they felt warm together and true. He had an urge to go further in this dream and court her right there and then on the sidewalk of some town long forgotten, he could take a knee and proffer a ring and live a thousand more moments just like this one through eternity, but his boyish excitement overcame him and he pulled away to suggest her meeting his mother. Before she could respond he was pulling her into the store his mother had just entered in an effort to find her and introduce her. The store was empty inside and he cried out for his mother but there was no one there. He turned to the woman to tell her his confusion but she had left as well. He looked at his empty hand which he was sure had held a good grip around her wrist, but there was no evidence that anyone had ever been with him.

As he turned to exit the store he noticed a note pinned to the wall. It expressed upmost regret and concern for those who came to view the last remaining remnants of the *Old Museum* and apologized in advance for those who were unable to leave. He pulled the note down and crumpled it up into a ball, spitting as he threw it out onto the street.

He walked for sometime in this dream, along the sidewalk and through the town, but there was no one left there and he soon woke up.

Ernesto expressed his condolences and shook the sergeant's hand before excusing himself to grab another drink from the bar.

At the bar stood Amelia Alda the hostess of this night's revelry chatting

with a nude Venus. The Venus wore nothing more than a red wig with faux hair
that reached to her toes. Ernesto bowed
to both of them and took Amelia's hand
in his to kiss her ring finger. The cor-
dial sentiment was accepted and he was
allowed to again stand. The Venus then
disappeared back into one of the many
sleeping rooms where guests went for
pleasure. It was just he and Amelia now
at the bar and Ernesto took the oppor-
tunity to look upon her. She was much
more beautiful up close than from afar
and Ernesto wanted to touch the soft
skin at the back of her neck, her golden
hair hanging ever so short entangling
his fingers. It was the same gold color
that she had been born with he guessed

and the thought of brushing it with his fingers sent shivers down his spine.

He turned towards her and putting out his hand to her asked, "Would you care to have this dance?"

"It would please me to do so, monsieur," she replied taking his hand.

They moved around the room stepping to and fro in each other's arms. She sang Love Poems into his ear and as he looked into her green eyes he saw her subservient, pleasure seeking nature. She smiled back at him with a warm smile like one a mother gives to her child after he has done something foul. He felt welcomed into her embrace and thought of never leaving its warmth and yet the song ended and they stepped away from

each other and she onto another partner
and he back to the bar.

Jane was at the bar waiting for
him. She was frowning.

"Did you enjoy your dance?"

"That woman casts a curious spell
over all men. I would try to explain it
to you but I can tell that you are jealous," he said.

"If I were jealous I would have
left. But I just can't see what you and
all these other mongrels see in her. She
looks pretty plain to me."

"She has a fair body and a simple
soul. These are the wants of men."

"And do I not possess a fair body
and simple soul?"

"You possess a fair body, yes. But your soul is much more complex," he said. "Now dance with me, dear. Before we run out of time."

"I think I'd rather not. You should go back to your blonde bitch if you want. I'm not interested."

As Jane walked away she passed Groucho who had been walking towards them and said, "Adieu."

"What does she mean by saying 'Adieu' so early?" Groucho asked when he reached Ernesto.

"The girl has a jealous heart, Groucho. She cannot deal with the desires of men and so she leaves"

"Ernesto, if you two have been fighting, I don't think it is wise to let her leave. Not with what she already knows. She may tell the police." Groucho had a wrinkle of seriousness in his brow. "I am not sitting in a prison cell because my friend steals a lady's heart as well as her purse."

"Come on, now. I wouldn't worry too much about her speaking to the police. She has enough of a record herself that it would be silly of her to turn herself in like that." Ernesto smiled. "Now what did you find around the house?"

Groucho sighed. "Ernesto, everything is as you said it would be. There is a small trap door in the master bedroom that leads to the roof. The roof is pretty well isolated. There are no sight lines from any of the neighboring

buildings. No one would have any idea
we were up there or what we were up to."

"Right. Now all we have left to do
is get Jones on the roof."

Ernesto Alvarez and Groucho Rex
sat on the edge of the roof skipping
stones into the open air while Jasper
Jones lay unconscious on his back behind them.

Ernesto said, "I can't believe you
had the nerve to club him over the head
like that. Don't you realize his guests
will be looking for him now?"

"Well, he said he was going to yell
out. We couldn't have all those Sleepers coming in on us with you holding a
pistol pointed at him. He called your

bluff, Ernesto. He knew your gun wasn't loaded. I had to do something."

"Wasn't loaded?" Ernesto fired his pistol up into the dark sky. It went off like a firework and echoed out into the night. "Wasn't loaded?" he repeated.

"Calm, Ernesto. He'll come to soon enough. Then we'll have it out of him. We'll have his art and his riches before long."

Ernesto walked over to where Jones lay and knelt down to check the rope around his wrists and legs. The bindings were tight and the man continued to breath, but would not stir.

"Well, I guess let's just wait and see," Ernesto finally said.

It was a little over twenty minutes before they heard a groan come from Jones.

"What happened?" he said, still lying down on his back.

Ernesto got up from where he sat nearby and kicked the man in the side.

"Allow me to introduce myself and my friend. My name is Ernesto Alvarez and this is Groucho Rex." He gestured towards Groucho who preferred to hide his face beneath the rim of his hat.

"I do not expect you to know us already," Ernesto continued. "But we know a whole lot about you, monsieur."

Jones spit blood before he said, "Look, you can have from the house what you want. I do not own anything of importance. I am a poor man. I own very little."

Groucho helped to pick Jones up onto his feet, which were still bound and leaned him against a wall.

Ernesto removed his pistol from its holster and again pointed it at Jones. "I think we maybe got off on the wrong foot here, monsieur. We are not thieves. We are not here to steal your physical wealth. We have come for much more, monsieur. We have come here to take away from you what makes you, you. Groucho, hit him once in the gut."

Groucho looked to Ernesto with some contempt but hit the man in his side. The man dropped, but Groucho picked him up and leaned him against the wall once more.

"See, that was a nasty trick you played on us earlier, Jones. We could have had this all settled and done with an hour ago, but you had to complicate matters by playing chicken."

"What? What do you want?" asked Jones, panting now.

"It's really very simple, Jones. We have some papers, you see. All you need to do is sign them. I won't explain to you what the papers say in depth but I can tell you some minor details. Your signature on these papers will give own-ership of the Jasper Jones name to me. You will no longer be legally allowed to host another dream exhibition under your roof from this night forward. In essence, I will become you and you will become no one and this whole creative empire that you have created in an effort to bring beauty to the world and reputation to yourself will now be owned by me."

"I don't think I understand, sir. How can you own another man's name?"

"Hit him again, Groucho. This time make it count."

"Why should I hit him again, Ernesto?" Groucho replied. "He looks pretty bad off already. Shouldn't we just get him to sign the papers and then be off?"

"Do what I tell you, Groucho. It's not your place to ask questions. Hit him again."

Groucho did not hit Jones, but instead began to untie the rope around his wrists.

"What are you doing? Do you want me to have to shoot you too?"

"What do you take me for, Ernesto? I'm not some ignorant crony that hits an unarmed man who is tied up just to do another's bidding. I'm letting him go."

"Stop right there or I'll shoot you both."

In the distance they could hear sirens. The three of them took pause to listen.

"Ernesto, I told you that you couldn't trust that girl. I'm getting out of here."

Groucho walked towards the ladder down to Jones's loft, but was stopped by two warning shots going past his front side. He turned to Ernesto and cursed at him.

"Neither of you can leave until I say you can," Ernesto said. "We still have some gentlemen's business to do. Now here Jones, here is a pen to sign these papers."

Jones took the papers and the pen in his bound hands and began to read through the text. Meanwhile, the sirens began to move closer and it sounded like they were only a few blocks away.

"We don't have time for this, Ernesto. Let me go at least. I don't want to be a part of this anymore," said Groucho.

"Fine, Groucho. I'll end it right here."

Ernesto cocked the pistol and fired. Both Groucho and Jones made an effort to duck but the pistol had not gone off. It was jammed. Groucho ran towards the ladder but Ernesto got to him first. They tumbled on the roof for a bit before finally Groucho pinned Ernesto with his own arm around his throat.

"Ernesto, enough is enough. It is time for me to go and time for you to stop entrapping me." Groucho loosened his hold. "Now, I will let you go, but you must no longer prevent me from leaving."

Groucho got up then and turned his back towards Ernesto as he walked towards the trap door. Ernesto cupped his throat for a moment gathering his breath. On his feet again he launched himself at Groucho. But Groucho had been expecting this and got a hold of Ernesto as he jumped at him. Using Ernesto's momentum Groucho threw him. For a moment in midair Ernesto looked asleep and then he rolled off the roof.

The police cars had still not reached the loft complex by the time Groucho was at the ground floor. He exited the building and ran to the convertible they had all driven in on. Sitting in the passenger seat was Jane Claulfield.

"Is he dead?" she asked.

"How did you know?" Groucho said.

"I felt it in my heart. I knew he was going to his death and there was no saving him from it."

Groucho went around the car and

climbed into the driver seat. "Where are we going?" he said.

"We can go anywhere, but let's not go anywhere that is like here."

"What about the seaside? Would you like it there?"

"Yes, I would like for us to go to the seaside. Please take us away from here."

A Midsummer Day's Dream

The cold waves of the lake reflect softly in the snow as the sun peaks out behind several clouds roasting the leaves on the trees to turn yellow green under pressure of draught. The snow falls without too much hesitancy and as it settles it turns the white tundra into a puddle of milky resolution creating streams and rivers that navigate the patchwork of the ground until finally coming to rest at the bottom of the cerulean body named Lake Chaubunagungamauganesha. It is hot as hell and the water boils sending steam into the air creating the fog of an outdoor sauna with entire landscapes melting in front of their eyes and time coming to a standstill each breath long thought out and constituting a lifetime's worth of memories and decidual attachment. Still the snow continues to fall and pile high covering them and their surroundings in frost-laden reminiscings looking freshly decadent while butterflies flock in the air one by one across the sky reputedly beating their wings gracefully rapidly imminently with flagrance in their small truculent hearts.

The group of three stops and admires the tree on fire in the woods. They whisper to each other.

"It's as if it doesn't even happen," says Hector Salvia his wooden pipe held between his back molars in an attempt accentuated by a hundred years beard that looks gristle.

Collette Trêveau steps over putting her hand into the fire swooning closer with her breasts first and then her pelvic region receding with warmth.

"The magic is in the crackle of the bark," she says.

They stand there with their bodies half submerged in the cool ice of the lake treading water and blowing condensed vapor from their parched lips in awe of sensation. Hector and Collette perched upon giant infinitely ancient stones stand fully clothed while Thomas Venireal kneels in a more naked form than any man before him has ever dared to betray. His cock held in both his hands ejaculating violet translucence upon the eddies beneath their feet. Mutters tuttered fruth with hith moth tin tones uf sublime. His masturbation raucousing paradoxical paroxysm pefore him within him surround him onto him sewing him new seeds to pleet his estimations succsexually birthed inground.

The timbre cabin lie before them. Its walls made of repurposed driftwood gathered between years stoopishly shushingtingly shorereal. They three the dream laborers of thine wooden shrine. Its casting made in mud and painted putty dyed the colors of berries picked lakeside. Within the floor is pastorurally divine. No inner walls and thousands of open windows to look through. The beds made of hay display simplicitlay a good lay. Dreams come withering true. The roof open but not for the snow to get through only at night for stars to shoot into.

"We should go back," says Hector, now sitting upon the cradle of a dead tree hanging atop an earthen, bunker shaped hill.

The water turns the color of Thomas Venireal as he swims ashore coming in human ether that bargained him his first respirior. Tither tin town tone time till twee tump to ta tland. To use to teveryone telling te to tuck off. His feet take to the heathen burn of the snow in two steps that indignate his spine in thrust worthy patience pelvis spanning three or four centimeters forwards then back finding no barrier to rub upontoin erratic juxtaposition. His cock hanging half limp in a forgetful manner of its own dripping continuum both violet and now turquoise with molden brazenness against the plain canvas beneath him.

Collette has half thoughts of tasting his expulsions as they swaddle the air from his penis painting the ground magenta vibrances. She reaches her smoking hand down now along her pale breasts touching the navel navigating the soft mound of wool down even further the fire churns embers between her thighs feeling alright. Her septum pierced nose follows and lowers quietly until she stands now folded over unto herself splicing splacking getting some goldish scarlet tail between her teeth chuttering shuttering slopping swallowing the elixir sopping she eventually self immolating and from the ashes now rising with blushing plumage now frolicking indefinitely.

"We should go back," says Hector.

He chops wood with a handmade axe of readymade cast iron. Collette helps him to build a fire. Thomas Venireal washes his paintbrush and leaves it to dry on a stone in the sun. He finds his robe hanging from the clothesline between two branches. They drink freshly steamed tea. The vapors evaporate in front of them cleansing the air further surrounding them. Their eyes relax a little bit and the vibrosity dulls. Everything becomes wet as the snow ceases to be.

"Now that we are here," says Hector. "Lets take the time to thank the sun."

Before them the sun spins its globes of fire turning orange and red in the wind disappearing beneath the tree line. The three of them stand by and watch in awe as the clouds turn pink and yellow in reflection of an evening onset of dark navy blues and blacks.

Hector reaches for Collette and the two of them embrace in the dark laying down now into the earth with limbs entangled. As they lay there Hector's long hair grows more brambled by the moment extending out through the grasswork into nearby shrubs and up the roots of trees becoming part of the surroundings as Collette straddles his waist placing her hand on his chest and pushing down with her hips as he pushes himself into her growing deeper inside of her with all of his branches extending outwards and upwards with solid motions of pelvic rapture. Their breathing gets heavy pocketing the air with moan-like son ambulance and the ground stirs with their kicks and swinging pendulance out back and forth up and down coming now all throughout the ground making the trees ejaculate with thick sap dripping down the bark and into the dirt as they roll around completing each other's every ecstasy.

Collette stands up onto her feet and begins to prod at the campfire with a long earthen rod and the white come from the fire spewing sparks upwards into the breeze burning bright as they splatter across the black canvas of sky creating a patchwork of jism dotted puddles of small burning stars brightening the darkness above with ecstatic white light glow.

Hector comes and goes and begins to sleep with his body now spread deep into the wilderness to be trod on with soft steps and moments of dream. He disappears as his beard grows leaves and his penis becomes nothing more than an inanimate piece of stone beneath a hill that rises with each snore.

Thomas Venireal returns from the lake with three freshly caught trout. He throws them onto the fire and they steam and wriggle in the flames with delight their skin turning dark and ashen as it peels back revealing pink flesh. Thom's eyes light up as he picks each fish up and swallows it whole his erect penis now projecting out the side leg of his underpants. With his stomach full he travels into the cabin which is painted in ethereal tones with blue and greens and browns and magentas and sandstones swirling around the walls in motions that respond to one's eyes closed.

Collette waits for him in his bed of hay. She is naked and covered in sweat. Her breasts breath and he finds himself drawn by the sweet smell fermenting from between her legs her cunt beckoning for his tongue to penetrate its walls. She spreads her legs and he peers deep into the pink of her slit into the dark purple cavern using his fingers to dig deeper and spread her wider fastening his tongue to the small bud pulsating in front of him in cyclic motions with the labia lapping back at him filling his mouth with the sea and her moaning with every wave of ecstasy.

Her legs squeeze against his backside pushing nose into cunt opening wider allowing head first and eventually shoulders to be pulled into her. Thomas continues head spinning world twirling eyes shut shuffling around he licks laps laughs at her innards and her orgasm grows louder being unborn unto unassuming. He feels his arms and legs growing shorter and his head becoming smaller cranium softer his life rewinds in front of him his birth goes backwards is undone before him as he turns into a giant ejaculating ball of nothing.

Collette doesn't have time to ask herself where all the lovers in her

world have gone her body still pulsating with the rhythm of masturbations
manically sublime surreaction curling
into a ball of fire for the last ethers
of embryotic light shining with blushing erotic warmth symbiotic while the
walls of the cabin around her spin in
tie-dyed synchronistic manufacture. Her
body takes small loops around the room
in the hay as it levitates with unreal
energy and lasting dogma for bodhisat-
tva ritual unfettering bonds a dream-
like pedigree divine woman burning into
the sun as blue-orange flames leap out of
her womb onto the carpet and back into
the trees the stars burning brightly now
as the whole earth becomes one solid
white lighted bonfire with music spinning

around it in a dance made of bird-headed men and women flapping their wings in semicircles and somersaults up and down until they have reached into the sky and brought the crescent moon down onto the ground with a loud looming boom darkening the night light and again resurging the fire within burning atmosphere and forests creating the vapid vapor of black whorish singulair all throughout the cabin fading and individual divides gaining. Then she shuts her eye lids and for the first time falls asleep her eyes still wide.